BEAGLES

Valerie Bodden

CREATIVE
PAPERBACKS

published by Creative Paperbacks
P.O. Box 227, Mankato, Minnesota 56002
Creative Paperbacks is an imprint of
The Creative Company
www.thecreativecompany.us

design and production by
Christine Vanderbeek
art direction by Rita Marshall
printed in the United States of America

photographs by Alamy (AF archive, Farlap,
Stamp Collection), Dreamstime (Michelle
De Kock, Marazem, Vladimir Mudrovcic),
iStockphoto (Mariya Bibikova, ChrisAt, igorr1,
Eric Isselée, phudui, rusm), Shutterstock
(Tiplyashin Anatoly, Anneka, Chris Howey,
IrinaK, Eric Isselee, Erik Lam, Nejron Photo,
Neveshkin Nikolay, Viorel Sima, SmileStudio,
Nikolai Tsvetkov, WilleeCole)

library of congress
cataloging-in-publication data
Bodden, Valerie.
Beagles / Valerie Bodden.
p. cm. — (Fetch!)
SUMMARY: A brief overview of the physical char-
acteristics, personality traits, and habits of the
beagle breed, as well as descriptions of famous
pop-culture beagles such as Snoopy.
Includes index.

ISBN 978-1-60818-360-9 (hardcover)
ISBN 978-0-89812-939-7 (pbk)
1. Beagle (Dog breed)—Juvenile literature.
I. Title.
SF429.B3B63 2014
636.753'7—dc23   2013005511

first edition
9 8 7 6 5 4 3 2 1

TABLE OF CONTENTS

Fetch!

FRIENDLY BEAGLES

A beagle is a *breed* of dog. Beagles are friendly. They love to cuddle with their owners. Beagles are *curious*, too. If they smell something, they will follow their nose!

WHAT DO BEAGLES LOOK LIKE?

There are two kinds of beagles. One is only about as tall as a ruler. The other is a little bit bigger. Most beagles weigh between 20 and 30 pounds (9–14 kg). All beagles have big eyes and long ears. They have big *nostrils* to give them a good sense of smell. Beagles' tails stick up in the air.

Adult beagles are 13 to 15 inches (33–38 cm) tall.

Many beagles are black, light brown, and white. These beagles are called tri-color beagles. Other beagles are red and white or light brown and white. Beagles have short fur.

BEAGLE PUPPIES

Newborn beagle puppies weigh less than one pound (0.5 kg). Tri-color puppies are usually only black and white when they are born. Some of the black areas turn brown when the puppies get older.

Young beagle puppies sleep for most of the day.

BEAGLES IN CARTOONS

Beagles are in many movies and cartoons. In the Garfield cartoons, Odie is a beagle. The Beagle Boys is a group of beagles that tries to rob Scrooge McDuck in Disney cartoons.

Garfield and Odie (left) are owned by Jon Arbuckle.

BEAGLES AND PEOPLE

People have been using beagles to hunt rabbits for more than 500 years. Today, many beagles are used as *therapy dogs*. Beagles also use their noses to help police find *illegal* plants and animals.

Using beagles to hunt is called "beagling."

Beagles are very good with kids. Beagle puppies can make good pets. But they are very active, and they can make a lot of noise. Adult beagles are calmer. But they might have learned some bad habits. Both male and female beagles make good pets.

Beagles will chew on anything if they do not have a toy.

WHAT DO BEAGLES LIKE TO DO?

Beagles can live inside or outside. They need to get some exercise every day. When beagles go outside, they need to be in a fenced yard or on a leash. Otherwise, they might follow a scent and get lost.

Beagles like to play fetch and go for walks.

Fetch!

Beagles love to play with their owners. You can hide your beagle's favorite toy. Then, let your beagle use his nose to find it. You will both have lots of fun!

A FAMOUS BEAGLE

Snoopy is one of the most famous beagles in the world. He is Charlie Brown's pet dog in the comic strip "Peanuts." He has been in many *Charlie Brown* movies, too. Even though he is a dog, Snoopy thinks he is a person. He even walks on two legs. Instead of sleeping in his doghouse, Snoopy sleeps on top of it.

breed a kind of an animal with certain traits, such as long ears or a good nose

curious wanting to know more about things

illegal against the law

nostrils openings in the nose

therapy dogs dogs that help people who are sick or hurt by letting the people pet and enjoy them

READ MORE

Block, Marta Segal. *Beagles and Other Hounds*. Chicago: World Book, 2010.

Green, Sara. *Beagles*. Minneapolis: Bellwether Media, 2009.

Johnson, Jinny. *Beagle*. Mankato, Minn.: Smart Apple Media, 2013.

WEBSITES

Bailey's Responsible Dog Owner's Coloring Book
http://classic.akc.org/pdfs/public_education/coloring_book.pdf
Print out pictures to color, and learn more about caring for a pet dog.

Just Dog Breeds: Beagle
http://www.justdogbreeds.com/beagle.html
Learn more about beagles, and check out lots of beagle pictures.

Every effort has been made to ensure that these sites are suitable for children, that they have educational value, and that they contain no inappropriate material. However, because of the nature of the Internet, it is impossible to guarantee that these sites will remain active indefinitely or that their contents will not be altered.

INDEX